Nursies When The Sun Shines

www.nursiesbook.com

ISBN: 978-0-615-67531-2

To my beautiful nurslings
- KH

Baby, sweet baby,
it's sleepy time.

See out that window?
It's getting dark.
It's night time.

At night time, we snuggle together in our cozy bed.

Baby goes to sleep.
Mommy goes to sleep.
Nursies go to sleep... sleep, nursies, sleep.

If you wake up and it's dark out that window,
It's still night time, my baby.

At night time, we sleep.
Baby sleeps. Mommy sleeps.
Nursies sleep at night.

I'll hold you and love you while you drift back to sleep.
You'll have nursies when the sun shines.

When the sun beams
through that window,
It's morning time, my baby.

In the morning,
Baby wakes up.
Mommy wakes up.
Nursies wake up.

It's time for nursies!

We snuggle together in our cozy bed,
having nursies.
Nursies when the sun shines.

Lightning Source UK Ltd.
Milton Keynes UK
UKHW050325311222
414661UK00004B/23